Fancy NANCY

Fanciest Doll in the Universe

Written by Jane O'Connor • Illustrated by Robin Preiss Glasser

HARPER

An Imprint of HarperCollinsPublishers

To Margaret Anastas, the best
(if not fanciest) editor in the universe
—J.O'C.

For the whole FN team, but mostly
Margaret and Jeanne, with gratitude
—R.P.G.

Fancy Nancy: Fanciest Doll in the Universe
Text copyright © 2013 by Jane O'Connor
Illustrations copyright © 2013 by Robin Preiss Glasser

ISBN 978-0-06-170384-3 (trade bdg.)—ISBN 978-0-06-170385-0 (lib. bdg.)

The artist used ink pens, watercolor, and gouache on watercolor paper to create the illustrations for this book.

Typography by Jeanne L. Hogle

13 14 15 16 17 CG/WOR 10 9 8 7 6 5 4 3 2
❖
First Edition

Do you have siblings?
That's fancy for sisters or brothers.
I do. JoJo is my little sister.
My parents say she is a handful,
which is polite for really naughty.

One time she hid from Grandma in
the children's coats department.

Another time she poured Easter-egg dye
in her kiddie pool and dunked Frenchy in it.

Last summer she used up all of
Dad's shaving cream to make it snow.

But today she did something despicable—that's fancy for a billion times worse than bad.

JoJo gave Marabelle a tattoo! She used indelible marker. Indelible means permanent, and permanent means it won't ever come off. Never, ever.

"Marabelle asked for a tattoo," JoJo tells
Mom. "She wanted to look like a pirate, too."

"That's a big fat lie!" I shout.

JoJo gets a time-out.

Then my mom tries consoling me.
That's fancy for making me
feel better.

  "Nobody can see the
tattoo. Not with her
clothes on."

  "It doesn't matter.
I know it's there," I say.

"Would this make you feel better?" My mom shows me an ad in the newspaper. "A gala is a very fancy party," she explains. "All the girls will come with their dolls."

A gala?

"I guess it couldn't hurt," I tell Mom.

That afternoon, Marabelle and I try to decide what to wear to the gala. We are both partial to purple, which means it's just about our favorite color.

Later, I try to scrub off Marabelle's tattoo. But it is a
hopeless situation. That means absolutely nothing works.

I am still not on speaking terms with JoJo
when Mom and I leave the next morning.

Ooh la la! We arrive at the Ardsley Park Hotel.
It has a canopy and a red carpet out front.

Double ooh la la! The gala is in the grand ballroom. Although many dolls are wearing the same ensemble as Marabelle, she is the most beautiful by far. Marabelle is the fanciest doll in the universe.

Marabelle rides on the doll carousel. I wave and shout "Bonjour!" every time she comes around.

Then we wait in line at the photo booth to have our pictures taken.

Marabelle would love to go into the doll dress shop and try on ball gowns, but I am worried someone might see her tattoo.

Instead, Marabelle joins some other dolls for tea. She tells them her name is Marabelle Lavinia Chandelier and then says, "Enchantée, chérie." That's French for "Pleased to meet you, darling."

"It's time for our tea now," my mom tells me. I grab Marabelle and we sit at a big table loaded with delicacies. (That's fancy for fancy food.) I dab my lips with my napkin and try to remember to take dainty bites.

Soon a lady announces the raffle. "Everybody look under your saucers. Whoever has the winning ticket number will receive a History Doll gift certificate."

Alas, we do not win.
"Oh well, chérie," I say to Marabelle.
"We still had a marvelous time."

That's when I notice
something strange. Marabelle
is not looking at me. Well,
one of her eyes is. But the
other eye isn't. And . . .

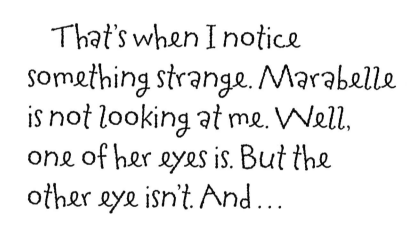

. . . lots of her hair is
missing in the back.

I duck down and take off Marabelle's dress. There's no tattoo! Right away, I come to a shocking conclusion. That means I realize something horrible has happened.

"Mom! This isn't Marabelle! This is somebody else's doll!"

People are starting to leave, but my mom tells me not to panic. She knows how to find Marabelle. I listen and say okay, because there really doesn't seem to be any other solution.

In a flash my mother rushes up to talk to the lady. "Attention, everybody. Kindly remain in your seats," the lady announces. "Two dolls have gotten mixed up. Will everyone please look to see if you have a doll with, er—with a drawing on her tummy?"

A moment later a girl cries, "Yipes! This isn't my doll. This doll has a tattoo!"

How mortifying for Marabelle. That's fancy for humiliating, which is fancy for very embarrassing.

The girl and I exchange dolls.

"My little brother cut off Lily's hair," she says. "And he poked out one of her eyes."

"Oh, I sympathize with you—I know exactly how you feel," I tell her. "My little sister gave Marabelle the tattoo."

On the way home I cover Marabelle's face with kisses. What a joyful reunion!
That means it's great being together again.

"Without the tattoo, we might not have found
Marabelle," my mom points out.
"Are you saying what JoJo did was good?
Because it wasn't. It was despicable!" I say.

"I understand," Mom says. "But JoJo won't always be so naughty. Little by little, she'll become more mature . . . she'll act grown up and responsible, like you."

Hmm. I hadn't thought about it that way before.

I guess I'm not the only girl whose sibling is a handful. And even though part of me is still a little mad, I accept JoJo's apology.

After all, it could have been worse. At least Marabelle isn't bald.